Storytime
for
3
year olds

by JOAN STIMSON

illustrated by
JOHN and CAROLINE ASTROP

Ladybird

No room for Panda

Lucy's Dad was a sailor. He sailed the world in a big ship. When he came home, he liked to bring presents.

One day Lucy's Dad sailed to China. When he came home, he brought a very special present. In fact you could say it was a *giant* present. Lucy's Dad had brought home a *panda*.

Lucy was thrilled. Her Mum was shocked.
She didn't know if they had room for a
panda.

That night Panda slept in Lucy's bed. It
was a bit of a squash.

Next day Lucy got ready for playgroup. She waited at the bus stop with Mum and Panda.

Panda stuck his paw out when the bus came. But the bus conductor was firm. 'Sorry,' he said. '*No pandas*. Panda's *too tall* for my bus.'

Mum, Lucy and Panda walked all the way to playgroup.

Panda shook hands with Miss Roberts. He was keen to join in.

But Panda got stuck – halfway down the playgroup slide.

Miss Roberts called the fire brigade. Then she called Lucy's Mum. 'I'm sorry,' she said. 'Panda's *too wide* for playgroup.'

Mum collected Lucy and Panda early. She decided to do some shopping.

Panda had never been to a supermarket. He wanted to ride in the trolley. But Panda was *too heavy*. He squashed the trolley flat.

'I'm sorry,' said the manager. 'Panda will have to shop somewhere else.'

Lucy trudged home with Mum and Panda. They told Dad all about it.

Lucy's Dad had a brainwave. 'Let's go swimming,' he said. 'There will be plenty of room for Panda.'

The swimming trip began well. Panda could swim like a fish. He gave the children rides on his back.

But Panda was *too frisky*. He made great waves in the pool.

The attendant blew his whistle. *'Time's up, Panda,'* he said. 'I'm getting soaked!'

Lucy's Mum helped to dry Panda.

Mum, Dad, Lucy and Panda started to walk home. On their way they passed the zoo. Panda tugged at Lucy's hand. He wanted to see the other animals.

The zookeeper smiled at Panda. *'No charge for pandas!'* he said.

Suddenly everyone knew what to do. Mum, Dad and Lucy agreed to leave Panda at the zoo. The keeper said they could visit whenever they wanted.

Panda looked round his new home. He liked the company. He liked the space.

Mum, Dad and Lucy waved goodbye for today. Then they went home – on the bus!

The duck who didn't like rain

The duck who didn't like rain

Derek was a new duckling. He lived with his family by the Big Pond.

Mr and Mrs Duck were proud of their ducklings. Every morning they took them for a long walk.

It was a long, dry spring that year. But at last it rained. And that's when the trouble started.

Mrs Duck was excited to see the rain. She lifted her wing carefully and woke the ducklings. 'Look, children,' she said. 'It's a lovely wet day!'

The ducklings rubbed the sleep from their eyes. 'Is that the rain you told us about, Mum?' they asked. They beeped with excitement.

'Let us proceed,' cried Mr Duck. The
Duck family set off in a long line. But Derek
lagged behind.

'What is it, dear?' asked his mother kindly.

'Don't like it,' said Derek in a small voice.
'Don't like the rain. Makes my toes feel tickly.'

'*Makes your toes feel tickly!*' cried Derek's

father. 'Whoever heard of a duckling with tickly toes?'

Mrs Duck didn't shout. That evening she paid a visit to Old Ma Goat. Ma Goat kept a shop. She sold most things.

Mrs Duck was in luck. The old goat had some wellingtons – just the right size for Derek.

Next time it rained, Mrs Duck gave Derek the wellingtons.

'Let us depart,' cried Mr Duck.

'How's that, Derek?' asked Mrs Duck kindly.

'Still don't like it,' whispered Derek. 'Musses up my feathers, spoils my hair.'

'*Spoils your hair!*' cried Derek's father. He was very upset to have a son who worried about his hair.

Mrs Duck went to Old Ma Goat again.
What luck! She had a smart cape and hood –
just the right size for Derek.

Next time it rained the Duck family
shouted cheerfully, 'Hurry up, Derek. Put on
your cape and wellingtons.'

'How's that, dear?' asked Mrs Duck.

'It's *lovely*, Mum,' replied Derek.

Suddenly he saw a huge rainbow. 'What's that, Dad?' asked Derek.

'*That*, my boy,' said his father, 'is a rainbow. A rainbow comes when the sun tries to shine through the rain.'

'It's *lovely*, Dad,' said Derek. He gazed up at the bright colours. He looked around in

wonder. Everything *sparkled* in the rain.

After that Derek wanted it to rain every day. He didn't always see a rainbow. But he loved exploring in the rain.

And sometimes he was in such a hurry that he even forgot to put on his cape and wellingtons.

Desert island friends

If I were on a desert isle
I'd like to take with me,
A PARROT who would squawk and chat
And keep me company.

If I were on a desert isle
I'd like to take with me,
A CHESHIRE CAT to grin and purr
And snuggle on my knee.

If I were on a desert isle
I'd like to take with me,
A LEOPARD with some spots to count
As carefully as can be.

If I were on a desert isle
I'd like to take with me,
A DOG who'd drag me off for walks
And chase me by the sea.

If I were on a desert isle
I'd like to take with me,
A HIPPO who would splash and swim
And make mud pies for me.

If I were on a desert isle
I'd like to take with me,
A GIRAFFE to reach down coconuts
For me to have for tea.

If I were on a desert isle
I'd like to take with me,
A DINOSAUR who'd scare me stiff!
BUT STILL BE FUN FOR ME.

Ready
at last

Ready at last

It was a lovely sunny day. The Fleece family were off to the sea.

'Hurry up, Cyril, hurry up, Susan,' called Mr Fleece. Mrs Fleece dressed the baby.

Everyone jumped into the car.

'*Baa, baa-tishoo!*' said Cyril. Cyril wiped his nose on his sleeve.

'For heaven's sake, Cyril!' said Mrs Fleece. 'Go back and fetch a hankie.'

Cyril shot upstairs.

'Baa, baa-tter get my book,' said Susan.

'Well, do hurry up!' said Mrs Fleece.
'I don't know why you have to read in the car.'

Susan shot indoors.

'*Baa, baa, baa,*' bleated the baby.

'Now, don't you start!' cried Mrs Fleece.
"I suppose you want your bottle. I've never
known a lamb drink so much.'

Mrs Fleece dashed into the kitchen.

Cyril, Susan and Mrs Fleece jumped back into the car.

'*Is everyone ready?*' cried Mr Fleece.

Cyril, Susan and Mrs Fleece nodded. The baby burped.

'Well, let's go,' said Mr Fleece. 'Or we'll *never* get to the sea!'

Nigel's toothache

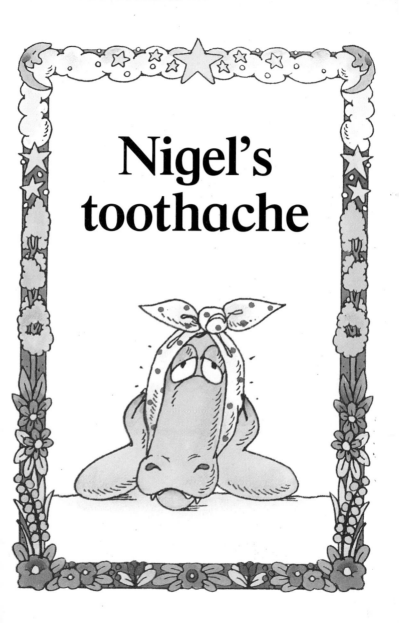

Nigel's toothache

Ben had a pet crocodile. The crocodile was called Nigel. Nigel was a very well behaved pet.

He kept his room clean. He wiped his feet. He ate up all his meals, but he liked cherry pie best.

One day Nigel didn't feel well. He left his egg at breakfast. He didn't want to play. Nigel had toothache.

Ben's Mum rang the dentist. Nigel went upstairs to clean his teeth. He jumped into the bath and turned on the tap. He scrubbed his teeth with a carpet brush. It was just the right size for Nigel.

Ben, Mum and Nigel set off for the dentist.

'Sit down, Nigel,' said Mr Webb kindly.
He tucked a napkin under Nigel's chin.
'Now, what seems to be the trouble?'

Nigel shook his head sadly.

The nurse passed a small mirror to
Mr Webb.

'Open wide, Nigel,' said Mr Webb.

Nigel did as he was told.

Mr Webb jumped back in alarm. He'd never seen inside such a big mouth before. He'd never seen so many teeth. 'Thank you, Nigel,' said Mr Webb. 'You can close your mouth now.'

Mr Webb looked at his little mirror. He looked at his small instruments. He looked down at Nigel and scratched his head. Then he had an idea.

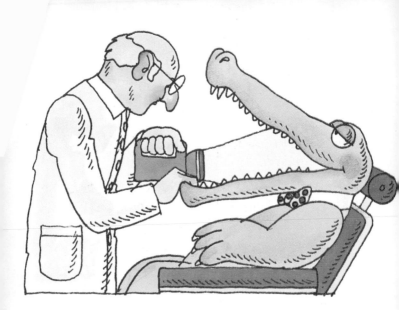

He sent the nurse out to his car. He asked her to fetch his tool kit.

'These look more like Nigel's size,' he said. He laid out all the tools. Then he said, 'Open wide, Nigel.' He knew what to expect this time.

Mr Webb shone his big garage torch into Nigel's mouth.

'Mmmm,' he said. 'What lovely clean teeth!'

'*Aaah*,' said Nigel.

Mr Webb prodded Nigel's back teeth gently with a screwdriver.

'*Aaah*,' said Nigel.

Mr Webb tapped Nigel's front teeth gently with a mallet.

'*Aaah*,' said Nigel.

'*Now* I can see the trouble,' said Mr Webb. He reached for his pliers.

'*Got it*!' said Mr Webb. He pulled a big cherry stone from between Nigel's teeth.

'*Aaah! Oooh! Mmmm!*' said Nigel. That was much more comfortable.

The nurse gave Nigel a pink fizzy drink.

'Rinse, please, Nigel,' said Mr Webb.

Ben, Mum and Nigel set off for home.

Nigel was beginning to feel hungry. They all went into the supermarket. Nigel pointed to one of the shelves.

On it were some tins and a big notice. '*New in,*' it said. '*Cherry pie filling… with no stones!*'

Indoor sports

Indoor sports

It was freezing cold in the sea. Mrs Penguin was worried.

Clive had a cough. Brenda had a sore throat.

'No swimming today,' said Mum firmly.

The penguins burst into tears. Clive had just learnt to float on his back. Brenda had a new beach ball. 'We don't want to stay indoors,' they wailed.

'And I don't want you under my feet,' thought Mrs Penguin. Then she had an idea. 'There's plenty of hot water,' she said. 'You can play in the bath.'

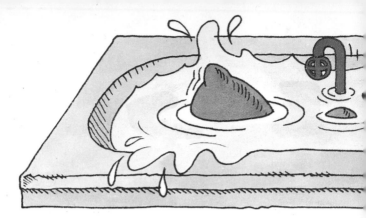

Clive lay on his back and flapped his wings. Brenda dived for the soap. Then she fetched her ball.

Clive and Brenda had a competition – to see who could make the biggest waves.

The morning passed quickly.

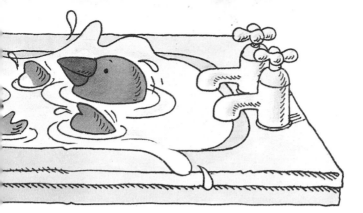

'*Lunch time*,' called Mrs Penguin.

The children rushed down in bath wraps.

'Have you emptied the bath?' asked
Mrs Penguin.

'Yes, Mum,' said Clive.

'Yes, Mum,' said Brenda. 'And we didn't
even pull out the plug!'

Hard work for elephants

Knees bend, arms stretch,
Reach right up to the sky.
Wiggle your trunks, flap your ears –
I DON'T believe you try!

Knees FLAT, arms stretch,
Struggle to touch your toes.
Back on your feet, jump up high
It's NOT the time to doze!

Knees bend, arms stretch,
This really should be fun.
Hop on one leg, clap your hands,
I'll MAKE you earn that bun!

Contents

Ladybird books are widely available, but in case of
difficulty may be ordered by post or telephone from:

Ladybird Books – Cash Sales Department
Littlegate Road Paignton Devon TQ3 3BE
Telephone 0803 554761

A catalogue record for this book is available
from the British Library

Published by Ladybird Books Ltd Loughborough Leicestershire UK
Ladybird Books Inc Auburn Maine 04210 USA

© LADYBIRD BOOKS LTD 1988   This edition 1994